Crap Ghosts

second apparition

Gavin Inglis

to poor Clare

Gavin Inglis

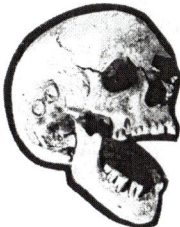

SKELETON PRESS

First published in 2004 by Bloc Press, Edinburgh

© Gavin Inglis 2004

This second edition first published 2007 by Skeleton Press

SKELETON PRESS

www.skeletonpress.com

ISBN 978-1-906252-00-7

Printed and bound by
Henry Ling Ltd, Dorchester, UK

Contents

Introduction
by Lynn Holden BA PhD

Perhaps the very ontological state of revenance is a mark of failure: unable to cross the border to the afterlife, the ghost is trapped in a liminal zone, no longer alive, yet unsuccessfully dead. The apparition, it must be said, is not always to blame—like Patroclus in Homer's *Iliad*, a spirit may be unable to pass through the gates of Hades if the burial rites are inadequate or if it fails the underworld's immigration inspections. In a nightmare of Chinese chthonic bureaucracy, a female ghost who has suffered a violent death is forced to obtain a special pass with an official seal before entry is permitted.[1]

Sometimes, though, the spectre is definitely to blame. Buddhists believe reincarnations are determined by one's *karma*, so a sinner is punished for a morally impure life by returning as a hungry ghost, or *preta*, forced to wander the earth forever starving, eating excrement, corpses and other foul things.[2]

---

1. Yüan Mei. "An Imprisoned Ghost" in *Censored by Confucius: Ghost Stories by Yüan Mei.* 1996. Edited and trans. by K. Louie and L. Edwards. Armonk, N.Y.; London: M.E. Sharpe.
2. Buddhist scriptures refer to sixty-four types of *preta.* Known to Japanese Buddhists as *gaki.*

Even when the external influences are favourable, a spirit may be unable to rest because of the physical discomfort caused by a flooded coffin, severe pain, or a lack of clothes—or the mental torments of guilt, greed and a craving for revenge.[3] And sometimes, as in the Greek tale of Philinnion who returns, though dead, to seduce her lover, it is a burning desire for erotic satisfaction that prompts the haunting.[4]

To add to a revenant's unease, failure to settle happily in the afterlife is often compounded by an astounding incompetence in mastering the art of haunting. Sometimes the spirit is not even scary—a mortifying trait in a ghost. The imperturbable Chinese sage Ruan Deru, when confronted in the privy by a ten-foot tall, black, fearful phantom, merely laughs, remarking that he has always heard that ghosts are hideous and now he can see it is true. What can the spectre do but blush furiously and flee?[5] In Oscar Wilde's eponymous tale, the Canterville ghost is unable to frighten a brash American minister and his family who offer this refined, if incorporeal, resident of an English stately home "Rising Sun Lubricator" to oil his chains. Nor is the family impressed by the recurring "bloodstain" on the carpet, for which the ghost has to steal paints from the daughter's box, resorting, when all the reds are empty, to emerald green and chrome yellow.[6]

---

3. A flooded coffin is mentioned in the Chinese text *Soushen ji*, and severe pain in *Xu Qi Xie ji*. A lack of clothes recalls a tale mentioned by Herodotus in which the Corinthian tyrant, Periander, summons up his dead wife to help him find something and she is cold and angry because he has neglected to cremate her clothes and has made love to her corpse.

4. *Phlegon of Tralles' Book of Marvels*. 1996. Trans. and intro. William Hanson. Exeter: University of Exeter Press. Page 68.

5. *Gu xiaoshuo gouchen. Youming lu.* Lu Xun.

6. Wilde, Oscar. "The Canterville Ghost".

Though a ghost may learn how to scare, an innate stupidity is harder to rectify, and here even an old ghost can be duped. When a phantom is asked by Song Dingbo—a counterfeit ghost who pretends to be recently deceased—what it is that ghosts fear, the spirit, like the biblical Samson, is caught off-guard and unwittingly replies that ghosts fear being spat at. The trickster Dingbo immediately throws the ghost over his shoulder, and when it turns into a sheep, he spits on it, to prevent it changing shape, and sells it in the market for one thousand five hundred coins.[7] In another instance, a ghost who starts to throw coins at a man is taunted: "Anyone can throw small coins, but I bet you can't throw large ones". Needless to say, the man grows rich.[8]

If incompetence seems to spook the lives of ghosts, it is pertinent to question its value; to investigate, in other words, the uses of inadequacy. Certainly, the terrors of the grave are mitigated by the comic misfortunes of those who return. Shortly before the Cultural Revolution in China, a collection of ghost stories appeared with the title *Stories About Not Being Afraid of Ghosts*. In the introduction, ghosts are interpreted as allegories of the iniquitous forces of capitalism and materialism, mere phantoms that will vanish if one's will is strong.[9] There follows a sequence of stories showing just how stupid spirits are, and how easily tricked. More recently, the sinologist Robert Campany, writing of the fallibility of ghosts, concludes:

---

7. *Lieyi zhuan.*
8. *Shuyi ji.*
9. 1961. Institute of Literature of the Chinese Academy of Sciences. Translated by Yang Hsien-yi and Gladys Lang.

The net effect of all these tales is to close
the moral and psychological gap between
living and dead persons, to emphasise ...
the continuing "humanity" of the dead.[10]

So ghosts are, after all, only human. It may even be true
for the dead, as it is for the living, that as the philosopher
Ludwig Wittgenstein states in praise of folly, "Our greatest
stupidities may be very wise."[11]

This paradox is not lost on Gavin Inglis. In this
wonderfully iconoclastic collection of ghostly tales, Inglis
charts the follies and fiascos, the adventures and mis-
adventures of poltergeists and revenants. Gavin's spirits
haunt the realms of failure, with communication lines
between this world and the other irremediably jinxed. In
their inventiveness and assured tone, these stories are a
fine contribution to the hallowed tradition of the
humorous ghost story that stretches from ancient China to
Oscar Wilde, John Kedrick Bangs and modern films like
Beetlejuice.

---

10. Campany, Robert. 1996. *Strange Writing: Anomaly Accounts in Early Medieval China*. State University of New York. Page 362.
11. Wittgenstein, Ludwig. 1941. *Culture and Value*. (originally published as Vermischte Bemerkungen). Oxford: Blackwell, 1998. Edited by Georg Henrik von Wright. Page 45e.

Beyond the Grave

"Your mother has one last thing to say to you, about the morning Aunt Filly died. The morning she didn't have enough for the bus ticket, and she got to the hospital too late to see her sister ... that one last time.

"She knows you took money from her purse that morning. You wanted to buy sweets. She knows all about it. She says you've to stop feeling guilty.

"You were just a daft wee girl then, and you've done many, many good things for people since. She forgives you with her whole heart, and you have to forgive yourself and get on with the caring work you're so good at. She says you've *always* ... been a wonderful daughter."

The girl collapsed to the stage, howling, eyes streaming with tears, letting out what sounded like decades of grief. The medium let her lie there for a moment before nodding gently to the wings. Burly security men helped the sobbing girl to her feet and returned her to her seat in the auditorium.

Pamela snorted. It was such an exhibition. She looked at the rapt audience around her, some clutching at their clothes, eyes shining in empathy with the poor girl who'd just been so publicly humiliated. It was *obvious* she had told somebody that story about her mother and the bus ticket, and the medium had got to hear about it. No great mystery. Pamela glared at Linda, who had dragged her here instead of the line dancing.

The medium took centre stage again, staring up to the ceiling. She was a young woman, a little dumpy, with vivid blue eyes. Lights swivelled to give her a shimmering halo.

"Thank you for being here tonight. We only have time for one more visitor from the other side." She descended from the stage and began to walk along the front row. "Does anyone recognise the name—" She suddenly paused. "Wait!" The medium looked towards Pamela and Linda. Then she approached them.

Pamela cringed inwardly. It was going to be Linda. She was always telling people her deepest secrets at the drop of a hat. This meant Pamela would spend the next three weeks listening to a wide-eyed Linda tell her There Was No Way the medium Could Have Possibly Known.

But the woman stopped in front of Pamela.

"You," she said. "You have a light above your head." Linda gasped.

"I don't think so," Pamela said.

"Oh yes." The medium's eyes were wide and compelling. "Please. Join me on stage." She lifted an arm.

Pamela shook her head, but a round of applause began and she had no choice but to troop out in front of everybody. She covered her face with a hand in shame. The medium told her to sit down facing the audience. White light shone in her eyes. It felt like an interrogation. She was giving away nothing to this woman.

"There is someone here who wishes ... to talk with you," the medium intoned. The microphone relayed her words around the theatre. "Someone who was a companion to you ... over many years. Someone who was always there for you."

Pamela's thoughts raced. Please, not her mother. With that description, it couldn't be her husband, thank God.

"His name starts with a 'C'. Something like Callum? Carlo? Charles?"

Pamela shook her head, feeling safe and smug.

"Charlie," the medium said, with finality. "His name is Charlie."

And all of a sudden, Pamela froze.

"I have a sense of someone outgoing, flamboyant and loud. Did you know a Charlie?"

"Yes." Pamela's voice went very quiet. "I did."

"And how did you know Charlie?"

Pamela felt a lump in her throat. "He was ... he was ... my *budgie*."

A ripple of amazement ran through the audience.

Pamela felt her eyes become damp. The words spilled from her. "He was always there for me at the end of a hard day. Always cheerful. Any time my friends let me down, he was there in the cage, whistling a happy tune, looking at himself in the mirror or ringing his wee ding-dong bell. He whistled me goodnight when I came with the cage cover. I..." Now she sobbed. "I *loved* that wee bird."

The medium laid her hand on Pamela's shoulder. "I can sense he loved you back. I can sense his gratitude for all the birdfeed and the tubes of water. And..." She looked Pamela directly in the eyes, "...he has a message for you."

"He does?" Pamela was aghast.

"Yes. A message that is terribly, terribly important for your future." The medium's eyes seemed to grow, to fill Pamela's vision. "I will attempt to relay it now." She straightened up, closed her eyes, and pursed her lips.

Then she whistled, a lively chirruping sound which lifted and trilled, dropping briefly into colourful piping. The spirit of the dead budgie spoke through the medium for thirty spellbinding seconds. Then she sighed, slumped a little and opened her eyes.

"What did he say?" Pamela urged.

The medium frowned. "I don't know," she said. "I can't speak Budgie."

Ghost of a Chance

I met this dead guy at the bar of the Golden Nugget, downtown Las Vegas. From the cut of his lounge suit, I guessed he'd been in the ground for twenty years.

"Thing about dyin'," he said, "you unnerstand life more. Like there are patterns in everything. Like a river follows soft ground, or a tree has rings because of the seasons. And though I never beat this casino, I come back now—take *charge* of that silver ball.

"See, I been studying the tables here, and this one wheel, each time it goes black-black red-red black-red red-red black, the next number—always 34. For five years it ain't missed once. I got my stack here," he uncovered twenty $100 chips which glistened with an eerie shimmer, "and I'm goin' down, get mahsel paid."

I took the floor with the dead man, and for three hours we waited for the magic sequence, through black and red, hi and lo, spin after spin after spin. And suddenly it was there, like footprints on a beach: black-black red-red black-red red-red black. He pushed forward his two thousand spooky dollars onto red 34, and we watched together as the wheel spun and the silver ball raced around the edge, plummeting in a perfect arc to rattle on the ridges between numbers.

Sure enough, it settled on 34.

"I told ya," said my friend. "I just made me seventy thousand sweet dollars, and I'm gonna park my ass here and wait for the same train again."

The croupier scooped in the losing bets, and I waited for him to award the dead man his winnings. But the croupier's wrist passed straight through my friend's tower of ghostly chips as if they weren't there.

"Shoot!" said the dead man.

Miner Apparition

Deborah had always been a little bit psychic. When the phone rang that morning, she knew it was bad news. She just knew it.

"Deb. Oh, Deb." It was Joan, and she was crying. A grip tightened on Deborah's heart. The two women were pit pals. Joan's husband was a twenty-year man. Deborah's own husband was long gone, but her son Billy had been working down the mine for eleven months.

"Joan? What is it?"

"There's been an accident."

Deborah's fingers stiffened, clutching the phone in a claw. "What's happened?"

"A cave-in. The worst they've ever had. An entire gallery obliterated. Obliterated, they said."

"Is Derek all right? Is *Billy* all right?"

Joan seemed not to hear. She spoke as though in a trance. "They got some warning. A couple of supports went and there was a minor fall. They got the call to evacuate the tunnel even as the big collapse started. They thought every man was out ... but one was missing."

"Your Derek?"

"No, Debs. He was with one group but there was a second shift working another face. He thought Billy was with this second shift and they thought he was with Derek. But when they did the roll call, Billy wasn't there."

"Oh God. You mean he's trapped?"

"Not trapped, Deb. They said ... they said nobody could have survived."

Deborah found she was sitting on the floor, with no memory of how she'd got there. Joan's voice was faint in her ear. "I'm so sorry, Deb. I'm so, so sorry."

The phone dropped from her hand. She stared at the honeysuckle wallpaper, the deep pile carpet in muted green, the cheap pine banister. Far underground, her son's broken body was lying alone, interred in a black, airless vault, crushed beneath a deluge of rock.

From upstairs came a slow, chilling creak. It was the sound of a door being eased open.

Nobody else was in the house.

When she looked up, Billy was standing there on the landing.

His face was gaunt, drawn. The morning sun from the stair window bathed his pale visage and unkempt, sandy hair.

Leading with his right foot, hand hovering above the banister, Deborah's son descended the stair towards her, step by silent step. She pressed back against the front door, drawing her knees up to her chest. His eyes seemed focused far beyond the walls of the house, focused on infinity. Deborah thrust a hand across her mouth to choke back a wail. One foot touched the ground, then the other. Billy drifted around the banister in a slow circle as his mother cowered beneath him. He disappeared into the lounge.

Deborah's instincts were to escape, to yank open the door and run screaming into the street. Yet this would be the last time she'd ever see her son. She forced herself up on trembling legs and followed him.

Billy was wandering around the kitchen, as if searching for something. She gripped the door frame and watched him. He looked aimless, lost, until his eyes came to rest on her. His mouth opened.

Deborah shivered uncontrollably. She knew she was about to hear a message from beyond.

"Got any eggs?" he said.

"What?"

"Eggs. Got any?"

"Was that what you wanted?" She couldn't help it. She began to cry. "Did you need me to be up more often, Billy, fixing your breakfast? Like when you were a wee boy? When you started at the pit, the shifts were so early. You said you didn't mind." She was howling now. "All these days, I slept while you were going out to work. I slept! All that time together we could have had. We could have talked. I'm sorry, Billy. I'm so sorry. I didn't know. I didn't know."

"It's OK, Mum." He looked startled. "Don't get upset."

"I know I should be happy for you, for where you're going. But it's hard for us, Billy. The ones who are left behind."

"Mum, I just want some scrambled eggs."

"I'll make them." She choked through her tears.

There were six new eggs in the fridge, beautiful big free range ones. She would make them with olive oil. Reaching for the pan, she bumped Billy.

"Sorry," she said. Then she froze. She clutched at his shoulder, his arm. He was solid. He was warm.

"Mum?"

"You're here. You're real. You're ... you."

"Stop being weird, Mum."

Now she looked hard at him. "What shift are you on today?"

"The..." He looked at the clock. "Oh, shit!"

Tea In The Attic

Grandma looked over the top of her glasses. "When I'm gone, this house will belong to you. And you'll probably want to sell it."

"Oh, Grandma," Barbara said. "You're not going anywhere."

The old lady lifted a hand. "*The Times* said a property was easier to sell if it was haunted. Well, this house *is* haunted."

"Really?"

"By my old china teapot."

Barbara sat back. "Uh, Grandma—'

"Your dear grandfather wasn't the first lover I had, child. During the war, a wounded French airman was brought here to recuperate. Pierre Duchamp was his name, and he had been shot twice in the leg. My mother gave him this attic room. She made a bed in that corner, so he could look out the window from where he lay. So he could see the sky. He stayed in bed most of the time—his wounds gave him terrible pain.

"It was my job, when I came home from the munitions

factory, to take him afternoon tea. I took up a tray with two cups, milk, a little sugar if we could spare it, and our china teapot with the curling pink fuchsia. I poured the tea, and we would sit and talk for a half hour. He helped me with my French language, and I helped him with his English.

"The poor man was still fighting the war in his dreams. At night, he would howl and cry out, delirious with fear. I couldn't bear it. I used to go up and comfort him. I talked softly in the darkness. And one of those nights, he pulled me close. He made a woman of me."

"God, Grandma! He took you by force?"

"Oh no, dear. I was twenty-two. I knew what I was doing. He was handsome, Pierre. And so raw, so, so ... male. But of course, it couldn't last. Mother found out, and the next day Pierre was banished. He promised to write, but his ship went down crossing the Channel. That very same day, the china teapot fell from its shelf and shattered into a hundred pieces.

"Some days, I come up here to think about Pierre, and what happened in this room. And sometimes..." Her eyes became misty. "Sometimes that old teapot will be there with its curling pink fuchsia. It sits where I used to place it, over there on the windowsill."

Barbara looked.

"Well, it's not there right *now,*" Grandma said irritably.

The Seaside Poltergeist

I used to be a sceptic. Any rational man is. In a long career investigating so-called psychic phenomena, I never encountered any happening that provided the merest proof of the supernatural. Never, that is, before the incident at Masonhead.

I was called in by a Mr Turner, who believed his clifftop house to be haunted, perhaps by a malignant sailor of times past who had died on the rocks far below. Mr Turner was much distressed when we spoke on the telephone; he described odd noises in the night and objects moving of their own volition. "I thought them poltergeists was supposed to pick on teenage girls," he said. "I've been living in this 'ouse by myself for fifteen year and I've never so much as brought a bird back."

I assured him there was a natural explanation and drove down there at once. The breeze was bracing, and I let my gaze wander as evening gathered across the bustling water of the Channel.

The moment I stepped over the threshold, I felt ill at ease. An awkwardness entered my movements, and I was grateful for the chair Mr Turner offered. I placed my phone on his table.

It slid across the surface in front of me, as if shifted by an unseen hand.

I grabbed it by reflex and stared at Mr Turner. He was on the other side of the room, his hands by his sides. I could see no way he could have interfered with my phone. Carefully, I restored it to its original place.

Smoothly, it repeated the eerie movement.

"You see?" said Mr Turner. "That's what it does."

"Good God," I whispered.

As evening became night, that was the least of the happenings I was to witness. Odd noises issued from one side of the house. Doors opened by themselves. Books toppled on shelves. Even the sofa would always slide to a certain spot on the wall unless prevented. And Mr Turner did nothing at any time; there were no threads, magnets or levers. I was at a loss to explain this unearthly behaviour.

Of course, I brought in the equipment and ran it through the hours of night. It was a frustrating session. There were no unusual radiations, no magnetic anomalies; only the occasional cold spot in a seemingly unrelated location. I was bewildered, and chilled.

For years I had derived comfort from rationality and always returned home secure in my latest explanation. Yet here was a demonstrable, reproducible anomaly which I simply could not account for. I felt utterly unbalanced. My throat dry, I explained this to Mr Turner, and promised to recruit other experts to help the poor man.

"Thanks anyway," he said. "Don't worry. You done your best."

Dawn had arrived and he accompanied me to my car.

We shook hands. I watched him return to the uncanny house, rubbing his head as he stooped beneath the doorjamb. My career was over, that much was certain. My confident explanations, my most basic assumptions about the world, lay in tatters.

As I started the car, I took a last look at this house, and shivered in the morning air. I knew I would never return there.

I also noticed that the house was at an incline of almost twenty-five degrees, tilted towards the cliff edge. I wondered if Mr Turner had informed his insurers.

Priestley Phantom

The conspirators gathered in a wayside inn. It seemed that each haunted face kept secrets, even from the others. When the innkeeper retired to bed, they met in the cellar and discussed what villainy they would commit next.

A pale apparition emerged from the wall. With an unearthly wail, it floated through the room lamenting the terrible tortures which the afterlife held for guilty souls. The petrified conspirators ran to the police station and made a full confession.

"I wonder why they turned themselves in?" said the first policeman.

"That's what happens," said the second, "when an inn spectre calls."

Haunted Hoover

Nick slid the Dyson out of its box. It came out smoothly, its virgin dust compartment gleaming perspex, the purple piping evoking exotic Continental architecture. He cracked the attachments from their individual cardboard compartments and fitted them into the base unit, jigsaw snug. He couldn't even tell what some of them did.

4.45 p.m. A couple of hours before Danielle was due. He plugged in the Dyson, took a last look at the untouched dust compartment and thumbed the power switch. The cyclone rose to a smooth hum and Nick eased it forward. The carpet became visibly lighter in its wake.

Ten minutes later, he finished the lounge and started on the hall. Halfway up, he met his previous vacuum, his mum's old Hoover, a steel upright with a rough grey dust bag. The first two letters had flaked from the fabric, so it now spelt OVER.

Nick carried it out to the street and set it down. He took a moment to look over its faithful but dated frame, channelling memories of his mother doing housework, swivelling in her apron while he played with wooden bricks or toy cars.

The Hoover had always frightened him; initially because of its loud noise, then through the more substantial fear that it might suck up his precious toys, disappearing them forever into its unknown interior. He suspected that several green plastic soldiers had been lost in action that way. Now the Hoover just made him think of his mother, long gone. Nick touched it one last time, then turned and headed up the stairs, ready to start cooking.

Later that evening, Danielle twirled fettucine on her fork and gave him a heavy-lidded smile. "You know there's an old vacuum cleaner beside your stair door?" she said. "A real antique. It's probably worth something."

"Really?" Nick was trying to remember where he'd put his condoms.

In the morning, she had to leave early. Her face loomed at him, the kiss coming out of the darkness. "You're such a Steptoe," she said. "Getting up in the middle of the night to pinch it. Good luck on eBay." Nick went back to sleep.

An hour later, he wandered into the living room with a bowl of Crunchy Nut Corn Flakes and the Hoover was there, in the centre of the floor, power flex wound unassumingly round its clips. He stared at it. Danielle had an odd sense of humour. He hoped he hadn't missed the binmen. On his way to work, he put the old Hoover out again.

That night, it was gone. Nick slept alone and dreamt of vortices, sucking holes in space that drew him in. For a moment he drifted awake, and thought he heard a distant, hollow howl.

The next day, he was possessed by the feeling that the old Hoover was in his house. He searched every cupboard, behind every curtain, under the bed. Nothing. He laughed at himself.

Drifting off later, he heard the sound of a motor. It was coming from his living room.

Drowsy, he stumbled through. There it was, the same old vacuum, plugged in and warm. With sleep-deprived focus, Nick got a kitchen knife, hacked off the plug, carried it downstairs and around the corner, and threw it into a skip. Back in bed, he stared at the ceiling and couldn't sleep.

Danielle came round again at the weekend. They watched a video, drank two bottles of Chardonnay, and fulfilled a sexual fantasy Nick had stored away since he was thirteen. Slumped together in the bed, sweaty and exhausted, they fell asleep, each breathing in time to the other's heartbeat.

Nick awoke suddenly. A distinctive whine came from the hall, drifting up and down, grinding as it hit an obstacle. The bedroom door, slightly ajar, let in a beam of light. Nick bit his knuckles as *a shadow moved across it.* The sound paused, raised in pitch, and came closer. Closer ... closer...

A grey shape nudged through the door. It was the Hoover, cleaning as it went, sucking hair from the carpet and wailing to itself. Nick jumped from the bed and stamped on the ON/OFF pedal. Nothing happened. He pounded his foot on it. Nothing. The power cable showed no sign of damage. He pulled the plug from the socket. Still the Hoover whined, sucking up dust, its appetite unsatisfied. It pulled at his hands.

"Nick?"

Danielle was sitting up in bed, wiping sleep from her eyes. "Why are you cleaning at this time in the morning?"

"I wasn't. The Hoover. It..." He gestured helplessly. The fan hummed to a stop.

"Is that the one you brought in from the street?"

"I threw it out. It ... came back. I have a Dyson."

He cast his eyes down the hall and gasped. The Dyson was in pieces, eviscerated. The piping was cracked, split, the cylinder shattered. The suction tube was mostly gone; all that was left were shreds.

Nick unzipped the Hoover's grey dust bag with tentative fingers. In the light from the hall, he saw mutilated pieces of expensive purple plastic, bedded in grime.

Danielle shivered in the doorway. "Why did you smash up your other vacuum?"

"I didn't. Why would I do that?"

"I don't know, Nick. That's why I'm asking you." Her voice had a dangerous edge.

"I *didn't.*"

"You think this is a good way to follow up what we did last night?"

"It wouldn't turn off. I pulled its plug out and it wouldn't turn off."

"That's enough, Nick." She reached for her top where it lay discarded. "Call me when you've finished being an idiot."

Dust mites swirled in the air behind her, picked out by delicate morning light spilling between the shutters. She slammed the door and he heard her stamp down the stairs.

Nick turned to the old vacuum. It sat there against the wall, innocently spelling OVER at him.

"Right," he said.

Way out of town, he parked beside a patch of waste ground. He wrestled the Hoover to a stony patch, then returned to the car for the can of petrol he'd bought from the twenty-four-hour garage. He unzipped the dust bag and poured a generous amount inside, fuel slopping from the heavy can. Then he switched to the exterior, soaking the bag, covering the cable, the handgrip, the base. Choking fumes filled his nose and mouth. Very carefully, he wiped his hands with a rag. Then he reached for the matches, struck one and threw it.

Flames leapt across the Hoover, feasting on the bag, dancing on the steel shaft. Thick black smoke billowed from the dirty interior, a column of death thrown into the sky like the last trail from a doomed aeroplane. Nick watched it burn, feeling suddenly tired and sad.

All day, Danielle wouldn't answer his calls. He had an early night.

Dreams in which little hairy beasts crawled over him tormented Nick through the small hours. An itchy nose eventually dragged him back to consciousness. It felt like he had a large moustache. He reached to scratch it with a sleepy hand.

His hand hit something hard and metal, about five inches from his face. Slowly he opened his eyes. Something dark and heavy was pressing down on his cheeks. Something bristly...

As if in slow motion, he heard the whine of a vacuum cleaner starting up, rising as the fan accelerated. Faintly, he smelt burning. Something sucked at his nose.

With both hands, Nick thrust the Hoover off his face. It crashed against the wardrobe, splitting the door. Its motor hit full speed and the vacuum cleaner blazed across the floor towards him.

Clad only in tartan boxer shorts, Nick wrestled the Hoover. They tumbled into the hall. He gave a samurai howl. It shrieked and whirred. Nick smelt hot dust.

He smashed the handle against a radiator. The base mashed his toes. He scrabbled for the zip of the dust bag. The vacuum tube encircled his wrist.

Together they lurched into the lounge, tearing a long strip from the wallpaper. Nick's head cracked against the door, but he tricked the Hoover with a two-handed throw. It toppled over the couch. He fell back, clutching his head, and pushed the door shut. He heard a series of bumps, then an angry humming from the carpet gap. Nick collapsed against the door, using his weight to keep it closed.

The minutes stretched into hours as he lay there in the darkened hall, shivering and woozy. The skirting board seemed to bend and bulge. Lines of green plastic soldiers marched past his mind's eye.

"Nick. Nick."

He blinked. Light streamed under the door. The living room was silent.

"Nick?"

It was Danielle's voice. She peered through the letterbox. He scrambled up and opened the front door.

"I saw that you called. I... You look like shit, Nick. Have you been up all night?"

He grabbed her and hugged her close.

"You're freezing. And you're shaking. What's wrong?"

He pointed a trembling finger at the living room. "The ... Hoover."

Danielle eased the lounge door open and stepped through. When she came back, she held the deadly appliance in one hand. She set it down in the stair. Her face was kind.

"Now you just do as I say," she soothed, and ushered him towards the bedroom. "You're exhausted. Here, lie down." She stroked his temple. "Get some sleep. I'm going to take the Hoover away, OK? You'll never have to see it again if you don't want to."

"But…"

"Sleep now." She kissed him on the forehead. "I'll check on you this afternoon."

Nick listened as she closed the front door, as her feet descended the stairs. Fingers pressed into his palms, he braced for the whine of the vacuum motor, awaited its next inexplicable attack. But seconds passed, then minutes, as he lay there under the warm duvet. The tension left his hands, then his arms, and he eventually slipped into a dreamless sleep.

When he awoke, it was dark outside. Yet Nick felt refreshed, relaxed even.

The clock said 9.00 p.m. Of course Danielle hadn't come back to check on him. When you found out you'd been dating a nutter, you didn't encourage them. Still, he was grateful for what she'd done. He should say thanks.

He dialed her mobile. It picked up on the third ring.

"Danielle?"

No voice answered him. But through the little speaker, distant on the line, there came a slow, eerie, hoovering.

Polterfife

—Mr McAndrew? You're the hotel manager? I'm Theo Goldberg from New York. *Spookervision.* We talked on the telephone.

—Oh aye. You're making the ghost documentary?

—That's right, sir. We got in last night. You still claim this is the most haunted hotel in the kingdom?

—Aye.

—More so than Sand Hutton in North Yorkshire? Than The White Swan in Harborne?

—I was talking about the Kingdom of Fife, like.

—Oh. Well ... we're doing a regional show right now, so that's just fine. Could you give an example of an unearthly occurrence that happens in your hotel?

—Sometimes I'm sitting in the bog, reading the paper, and I hear footsteps going up the stairs.

—In the middle of the night?

—Naw. After lunch.

—And what do you find when you get there? Any physical traces? Any unusual signs?

—Well, I'm in the bog, like, so I dinnae bother. But

sometimes they come back down and go oot the front door.

—I see. We need, ah ... something more visual for the programme. I hear you have a headless horseman?

—Aye. But he's no headless.

—He's just a horseman then?

—Naw. He's legless.

—He has no legs? How does he ride a horse?

—He's got legs. He just gets legless. In the pub, like.

—He gets drunk?

—Aye, he falls over and goes tae sleep on the floor.

—How do you know he's a horseman?

—Well, he wears one of they round hard hats like the bankers wear.

—A bowler hat? But horsemen don't wear bowler hats.

—Maybe he's no a horseman then.

—Mr McAndrew, I have serious reservations about this joint. Even your domestic standards are sloppy. My room has obviously not been cleaned for several days.

—That'll be the phantom maid then.

—You have a ghost for a housekeeper?

—Aye. Nobody ever sees her.

—But she makes up the rooms?

—Naw, she doesnae. It's very mysterious.

—Can you give me one actual example of a paranormal phenomenon that has happened in this hotel?

—Oh aye. Late last night, upstairs, I saw some queer things.

—Well, this is more like it. Would we be able to capture these on camera?

—Eh well, I doubt it. My wife and I had a fight and she poured drain cleaner into my bottle of Grouse. So that may have been responsible, like.

—Mr McAndrew, my team will be moving on this morning. We shan't stay for breakfast, and I won't be paying your bill. Hey! Where's our van? We parked right there by the door.

—Maybe you've fallen foul of the ghostly joyrider that haunts these parts.

—All our equipment was in that van! It's worth thousands of dollars!

—Aye, it's spooky how he knows when to strike.

Ghostly Benefactor

Miss Kingdom gave a short nod of satisfaction and slipped the glasses off the bridge of her nose. They settled on a cord as she gave the smart young lady in her office a searching glance.

"We're delighted to welcome you to the school, Miss Simons. You have a lot to offer the girls. And I very much look forward to seeing your innovative choreography in the Christmas show. But—" She hesitated. "There is one thing I must tell you. It may sound ... rather far-fetched."

Miss Simons smiled. "Five years of teaching leads one to expect the unexpected where young dancers are concerned."

The head teacher frowned. "You may not know that St Hilda's was originally a private residence. It belonged to a Mr Templeton, a kindly industrialist who was passionately interested in the theatre, and dance in particular. He had no family. I think, beneath the surface, he was a rather lonely old gentleman. When he passed away, his will instructed that the house be converted into a school of dance, and he provided a generous annuity to fund its activities. The only condition was that the school should make regular public performances to strengthen its links with the community. I was brought in as the first headmistress, and we have always complied with Mr Templeton's dying wish. But there is a further aspect to the story, one which may ... stretch my credibility."

The elderly teacher had been staring at the desk. Now she looked up at her new recruit.

"We think the school is haunted by the spirit of Mr. Templeton. There have been too many reports—nothing frightening or malicious, you understand—but he has been seen by several teachers. Always in the run up to a show."

The headmistress leaned close to Miss Simons, her voice dropping to a whisper. "During rehearsals, *he is sometimes there*. In the back row of the theatre. A gentleman, they all say. Well dressed. He watches the girls dance. If approached, he vanishes without a trace. I've lost more than one teacher to this ghost story, Miss Simons. I want you to know up front—and I hope it will not affect your decision to join us."

The young teacher smiled and offered her hand. "Naturally not."

So Miss Simons took up her duties, and largely forgot the story of the ghostly benefactor. It crossed her mind only once, when she first toured the little theatre. The rear stalls were draped in shadow, and she could altogether credit how a tired eye could play tricks there.

After weeks of studio work with clumsy young ballerinas, Miss Simons felt very much part of the school. She knew that she personally would be judged by the Christmas performance, and she drove the girls hard. In time, they moved rehearsals to the theatre itself. She was onstage, amidst the girls, when she first saw the man in the back row.

The lights were in her eyes, but she shaded them with a hand. It seemed that a figure, an elderly man in jacket and tie, was sitting in the rear stalls, watching the stage. Miss Simons froze as dancers paraded round her. Then she stepped down into the auditorium and walked decisively up the aisle. She was blind for precious seconds as her eyes adjusted to the darkness.

When she reached the back row, it was empty.

She searched the rows of seats. Nothing.

Miss Simons shivered.

Preparations for the show proceeded over the following weeks. Again and again, she saw the uncanny figure, the kindly old gentleman in the back row. Always he melted away at her approach, and in time, she ceased her attempts to confront the apparition.

On the night of the dress rehearsal, she was up in the gallery, rigging lights, when she saw the ghostly benefactor from her vantage point. He seemed so solid, so real, his eyes fixed on the stockinged young dancers onstage as they approximated *Swan Lake*. Slowly, Miss Simons realised that her gallery ran back to a stair behind the stalls. She determined to try one last time to witness the phantasm at close range.

Along the creaky boards of the gallery she tiptoed, down the groaning iron of the rear staircase. With a frown, she noticed that the ground-floor fire exit hung ajar. But through the auditorium doors, very close, she could see the old gentleman in the back row.

Miss Simons slipped inside, catlike, to get one good look

at the ghostly benefactor. He wore a suit of an archaic cut, and his tie hinted at the cobwebbed glamour of a bygone age. His eyes were fixed on the young dancers. She noticed he was not in fact motionless; he was directing something in his lap. She drew close to see.

The elderly gentleman had his trousers open and his penis out. It was red and swollen. He was masturbating furiously with one wrinkled hand.

Miss Simons gasped and clapped a hand to her mouth.

Startled, the old man sprang from his chair and threw himself over its back. He ran for the exit with distinctly solid footsteps, fumbling at his trousers all the while. Clattering against the fire door, he stumbled into the night, his breath steaming in the cold air.

The next day, Miss Simons approached the headmistress to have the locking mechanism of the fire exit repaired. Miss Kingdom was flushed with excitement and captivated by a small object on her desk.

"Incredible news, Miss Simons. The younger girls found *evidence* of our school spectre in the theatre. They scraped it from the seats themselves!"

She held up a tiny jar containing dull, sludgy fluid.

"Look! Ectoplasm."

Irreverent Revenant

At that time, it was the custom that a watch be kept on Edinburgh graveyards for resurrection men, who would steal the bodies. Kenneth Sim was on duty when he observed a dark figure slipping between the trees. He lit up a torch and pursued the interloper, pistol at the ready.

The trail ended beneath a great yew tree, where his light cast shadows like grasping fingers. Kenneth was shocked to see a wizened figure climbing into one of the fresh graves. It turned its head and gave him a ghastly look.

"Yes," it said, "I have risen from my resting place to go abroad by night. I have serious matters to resolve ere I can lie still."

"How ... how dare you profane this holy ground?" stuttered Kenneth.

"You do not understand, Kenneth Sim," hissed the revenant with a hideous, fractured smile. "Many mysteries are hidden from the living. Speak not of my movements, and I will make you a rich man."

"How will you do this?" asked Kenneth.

"Search the beach at Joppa. You will find a red rock with

seven sides. Buried beneath is a treasure that you can scarcely imagine." With that, the revenant lay down in his grave and scooped the earth back to cover his body.

Come morning, Kenneth made haste to Joppa. He found nothing at first, but persevered and at last came upon an odd flat red stone, with seven distinct sides. Fingers trembling on his spade, he dug deep into the sand beneath it.

After an hour he struck something solid and parted the sand to see. In horror, he realized that it was a human knee. Kenneth fled from the hole and collapsed on the grass nearby.

However, an image kept rising before his eyes: a priceless gem buried on the person of its owner. He gathered his courage and crept back to the hole. Gradually, he exposed more of his discovery: dry ankles, ribs draining of sand, a protruding collar bone. But no gem. Kenneth took a deep breath, and brushed the last sand away from the buried face.

"Surprise!" yelled the revenant, and leapt to his feet. He vaulted from the hole, gave a little dance, and, giggling, ran off down the beach.

The Phantom Pilot of Pentecost Island

"This is civilian flight November Golf Four Four Eight Bravo. Request ... emergency landing clearance." The greasy black radio crackled. "...injured. Storm coming."

Vilisi grabbed her mouthpiece. "November Eight Bravo, this is Sara Airfield. What is your condition? Over."

"Losing ... losing blood. Hard to concentrate. I'm all alone up here, Sara." It was an English voice, weak and distant.

"He sound like he had six shells of *kava*," old Ezekiel said.

Vilisi leaned back in her chair to look past the mountain. From the height of the wooden control tower, she could see dirty clouds looming towards the island, darkening the sea. She shook her head. "That storm front's coming up fast from the south. If he's in a small plane, he's only going to get one approach."

"Best keep him talk." Ezekiel nodded. "Long as you can."

Vilisi scanned the radar. "November Eight Bravo, our runway is clear. What is your ETA? Over."

"Seeing ... things, Sara. Shapes in the clouds. Faces..."

Vilisi grimaced and thumbed the transmit button again.

"Stay on the air, November Eight Bravo. Talk to us. We will bring you in. Over."

"Tired, Sara. Too tired..."

"November Eight Bravo. November Eight Bravo!"

The radio hissed for thirty seconds. Ezekiel shook his head, chewing on a strip of papaya skin.

Suddenly, the English voice was back, heavy and slurred. "There's somebody here now, Sara, in the cockpit with me. A ... boy. He's going to take the stick."

"You have a co-pilot, November Eight Bravo? Over."

"Never seen him ... before. Says his name is Kalkot Kalmari."

Ezekiel coughed. "Do he say ... Kalkot Kalmari?"

"Sounds like an islander."

"You never heard of him?"

Vilisi looked at the old man. "Should I have?"

"It twenty years ago. A small plane return from Fiji. Two passengers. The pilot take a stroke of the head. Collapse in the cockpit. All dead, for sure. But then ... a voice come over the radio. A brave young boy with no experience take the controls. His name is Kalkot Kalmari."

Vilisi stared at Ezekiel. Hairs tingled on the back of her neck. It was growing dark outside, the storm front bearing down upon the airfield. They had minutes left.

"November Eight Bravo, what is your status? Over."

There was a long pause before the drowsy voice responded. "The boy is taking over. I'm ... going to sleep now."

"Negative, November Eight Bravo. Stay awake. *Stay on the air.* Over."

Eerie static crackled through the tower. The air seemed electric, alive with tiny needles.

"Twenty years ago. What did this Kalkot Kalmari say?" Vilisi hissed. "What did he do?"

Old Ezekiel frowned, his glistening eyes focused beyond the walls of the tower, gazing into the past. "He take the stick. I describe the controls. My hands shaking. I tell him the artificial horizon, the air brakes. I talk him to level the plane and bring round for the runway. Then—"

Thunder shook the tower beneath their feet. Charts and coffee mugs crashed to the floor. Vilisi spun to see an immense fireball erupting from the side of the mountain. Black smoke billowed and pieces of grey fuselage rained on the forest, pieces that were the remains of November Golf Four Four Eight Bravo.

"Yup," said Ezekiel. "Twenty years ago, that *exactly* what he did."

Revenge on Regent Street

Rain lashed the windows. Lightning split the sky and thunder rolled across Soho like the end of days. My lights flickered and the balcony doors rattled in their housing. But that wasn't why I stood breathless, a cold finger on my spine. I was watching the thermometer. The temperature was dropping, dropping as smoothly as if the mercury were pouring out the bottom of the glass.

For weeks, I had sensed a chill malevolence gathering in my rooftop apartment. I had felt a presence in the building, a silent watcher within the walls. Of course, I had made enemies in the media business, in Whitehall, enemies within my own family. But I had faced nothing I couldn't fight or reason with. Nothing I couldn't buy.

My breath misted as I prowled the lounge. One by one, lights winked out, snuffed by the unseen intruder. I shivered and hugged myself against the fear. "What do you want?" I yelled.

Lightning painted the room, and as thunder shook the floor beneath me, I read the afterimage of a word, a word daubed in red on the mirror over the fireplace.

REVENGE.

My heart pounded. "Revenge for what?" I screamed. "Who are you?"

The lightning flashed again, and the gory word had changed.

JIMMY.

I blinked. "Jim Henderson the cameraman? The guy I smoke with out the back of the studio?"

"Noooo." The groan was slow, cavernous. It came from nowhere.

"Jim McManus from the Coach and Horses? The one that drinks Directors?"

"Nooooo!" Now there was distinct menace in the voice.

"Uh ... Jimmy ... Jimmy Wong?"

Cupboard doors flew open across the room and something tore from the shelves. It crashed on the floorboards, scattering yellowed cash and small, green houses.

It was my Monopoly set.

As I stared at it, a memory tickled at my brain. A memory of northern winters, a child's attic bedroom warmed only by a rickety fan heater. And long hours spent huddled over ... huddled over...

"Jimmy Wilson? From next door?"

"Ysssssssss." It sounded like a dying breath.

"That kid I used to beat at Monopoly?"

The cupboard doors slammed. The screen of my three grand television blew out. Wine glasses lifted from the table and smashed against the French windows.

"Those were fair games. It's not like I cheated."

There was an ominous silence.

"So ... what kind of revenge do you want?"

The Monopoly board lifted two inches and dropped back onto the floor.

"You want a *rematch?*"

Before my eyes, Monopoly money peeled from the box, drifting through the air to form two neat piles. The CHANCE and COMMUNITY CHEST cards executed a balletic aerial shuffle, and the dog and battleship floated over to land on GO. The dice began to dance in mid-air, shaken by an unseen, questioning hand.

"Be my guest," I said.

The dice rattled harshly on the board. A four and a five. The battleship slid forward to Pentonville Road.

"I always play the battleship," I said.

Angrily, the battleship exchanged places with the dog. The dice dropped in my lap and the game was on.

On my first go, I landed on the Angel Islington and tried to buy it. An unseen force slapped the title deeds out of my hand.

"Once round the board before you can buy anything," I murmured. It had been our rule, Jimmy and I. I had forgotten. While I wallowed in memories, he landed on COMMUNITY CHEST, his annuity matured and he received £100.

It was surprising how quickly I became absorbed in the game and forgot I was playing with a phantasmal force. Jimmy passed GO first and began to collect the pinks, oranges and yellows. I only got a couple of stations and Trafalgar Square before I got sent to jail and had to pay £50 to get out. I snagged Piccadilly to block him on the yellows and was celebrating an "Advance to Mayfair" when to my horror he landed on Bond Street and made his first set of three.

Things got serious. I made the set of light blues and filled up with houses, but he completed the oranges and the pinks. Worse, Regent Street began to exert a magnetic pull on my battleship. Every time I rounded the corner, it was £390 for two houses. And as he added a third, it went up to £900. When I rolled a third double from Fenchurch Street Station and went directly to jail, it seemed a mercy.

Fortunately, I completed the reds and Jimmy over-extended with his green property renovations. His hapless dog landed on the Strand for £700. I built the reds up to four houses. And on the very next roll, he drew "Advance to Trafalgar Square". I looked down at the title deed: £925.

The invisible Jimmy hurled the dice against the wall. He was £740 short. He would have to sell most of his houses. Quietly, I said, "I'll take Park Lane instead."

There was another long, ominous silence. Then the precious dark blue card flipped to the MORTGAGED side and £175 leapt from the bank into his pile. I thought he was going to clear himself out to raise cash—but the mortgaged property lifted in the air and slapped down in front of me. It was a cheap move. But I let him away with it.

After that, the excitement sagged. Regent Street got me again and I mortgaged a few stations. Fleet Street became a nice little earner and I got a few houses on the dark blues. More money flowed into the game every time we passed GO. Jimmy survived four houses on Park Lane. I handled a hotel on Regent Street. The night wore on, and I found my eyelids drooping. Jimmy's invisible movements appeared to have slowed too, and once I caught what I thought was an eerie yawn.

"You want to call it a draw?" I asked.

The storm had departed hours ago, but the house lights

flicked on and off so I could see a new red word on the mirror.

MAYBE, it read.

I rubbed my face. "How did you die, anyway?"

From the Monopoly box, the top hat and old boot rose together, a crude imitation of a person. They walked across the Free Parking square. The racing car slid along the board and knocked them in different directions.

"You were hit by a car?"

"YSSSSSSSSSS."

"Sorry to hear that."

Sadly, his money drifted back into the box. Silence pressed in around us.

"You want another game sometime? I mean, you're always welcome."

PROBABLY NOT, read the mirror.

"Well ... look after yourself." I stood up. As an afterthought, I added, "You would have got me in the end."

There was no answer. A window flapped in the kitchen. I felt that the spirit of Jimmy had departed. Idly, I rolled the dice for him one more time. Double two. COMMUNITY CHEST to Park Lane with a hotel.

No way did he have enough cash to cover that.

Ottomanifestation

Nigel lay back on the ratty couch and stretched out, soaking up the vibe. Thom's living room was very mellow. Woven Egyptian throws covered two walls, and the cheap rental-flat lamps were veiled with red and purple scarves. A hookah stood on the sideboard, its patterned hose curled around the pipe. The stereo pumped out exotic strings and flutes over tambourines and drums; one of those Rough Guide sampler CDs.

There was just one thing missing. Nigel felt down beside the sofa, and discovered something soft and velvety. He drew it into the light. It was a low octagonal footstool, aubergine-coloured, sagging on one side and bearing what looked like red wine stains. It had no feet, just eighteen inches of raw cushion. He lifted his legs and let his ankles rest on the top. They sank into the material. Perfect. Nigel let out a long, contented sigh.

Thom ambled back into the room, bearing two fruit beers. He handed one to Nigel and whistled. "Woah. You're taking a chance there, using that footstool. It's haunted."

Nigel didn't process this until Thom reached the armchair across the room. "Sorry... What?"

"Haunted, man. Possessed by the spirit of a dead Turk."

Nigel spluttered his beer. "What?"

"Yeah. From the fifteenth century."

"A five-hundred-year-old Turkish man has possessed your pouffe?"

Thom's face didn't change. "It's true." He drank his beer. "Technically, he's not five hundred years old. He's just been dead that long. Five hundred and fifty-five years, to be precise."

"So you know who he is?"

"Sure. Çandarlı Halil Pasha."

"What?"

"Çandarlı Halil Pasha. A grand vizier from the Ottoman Empire."

"He, uh, told you this?"

"No, man. It was one night. We worked it all out. We got together all the evidence and we looked it up on the Web."

"The Web told you a grand vizier was haunting your pouffe."

"Fuck's sake, Nigel. Open your mind." Thom sparked up a cigarette. "Evidence number one. This guy died five hundred and fifty-five years ago, in 1453. We know the exact date because he was executed. The Sultan, like, fucked off and left his kid in charge, so Çandarlı Halil Pasha had to look after the Empire. But every time the shit hit the fan, he called the original Sultan back. Eventually the kid grew up and got so fucked off with the situation that he just ordered the grand vizier's execution and took all his money."

"How is that evidence that he's in here?" Nigel thumped the pouffe with a foot.

"Those stains might be blood spatter from his execution."

"They're red wine. This pouffe is not five hundred years old."

"Yeah, but they might be, y'know, psychic stains. You haven't researched this stuff, man. There's this system called the Abjadi order of the Arabic letters, and five hundred and fifty-five in that spells TH-N-H."

"So?"

"What's my name?"

"Uh, Thomas Henderson."

"And my middle name?"

"I don't know."

"It's Nicholas. Thomas Nicholas Henderson. You see? TH-N-H."

Nigel stared at Thom. "I don't think that's enough evidence," he said finally.

"Well, evidence number two, pouffes are sometimes known as ottomans, and..." he cocked his head, listening, "...evidence number three is coming up right now. You better take your feet off our friend."

Nigel complied. The stereo was pumping out airy flute music, filling the room. Whether it was the beer, or Thom's sudden exhibition of considered insanity, Nigel felt light-headed. There seemed to be a vibration in the floor, a thrumming; perhaps a washing machine in the flat downstairs.

"This is Dervish prayer music," Thom said. "He loves it."

And before Nigel's eyes, the pouffe lifted smoothly from the ground and hung in space, a ten-inch gap between it and the floor.

"See, man? Haunted."

Gobsmacked, Nigel waved a hand beneath the pouffe, then above it, feeling for wires. The pouffe gently oscillated in time to the flute. Then, as a bank of hand drums rumbled into the recording, the footstool began to spin.

Thom smiled and nodded along, as the music and the pouffe gathered pace. "He can't get enough of it."

Nigel sat back and stared.

"It all makes perfect sense," Thom said. "The Dervish stuff is about, like, meditation. Ascetism. Vows of poverty and reaching religious ecstasy. That might well let you come back after death."

"You said this Ali Pasha guy was loaded."

"*Before* his death. After his death he was penniless."

"That's true of *everybody*."

"Never mind that." Thom eyed the gyrating footstool as it accelerated, the drums and flute driving it towards oblivion. "Are you ready?"

"Ready for what?"

Thom sprang from his chair and grabbed Nigel's shoulders. He dragged them onto the possessed pouffe. "PILE ON!"

"Wooooaarggh!" Nigel struggled, arms and legs flailing, like a starfish in a washing machine. Beer whirled inside his stomach.

"Yaaaaagh!" Thom giggled like a kid.

"Nooowrgn!"

"Gaaaargh!"

Nigel rolled across the floor and whumped against the sideboard. Glasses shattered inside. The hookah crashed down beside him. Thom soared across the couch and tumbled over its arm, landing arse-up beside the TV.

"You fucking idiot!"

Thom laughed harder. As the track wound down, the footstool slowed its rotation, steadied like a hovercraft, then finally sank to the ground. It sat there, inert, a plain old piece of purple furniture, stained and a bit loose at the seams.

Nigel blinked. "Your evidence number two is bollocks as well. That's not an ottoman. An ottoman's a big thing like a love seat. That's just a plain old pouffe."

Thom got to his feet and grinned. He went over to the hi-fi.

"Fair point, man. But will I put the track on again?"

Nigel glared at him. Then he snorted.

"Go on then."

Much, much later, they made the mistake of playing James Blunt.

Breathtaking Wonders of the Hidden Red Pavilion

Chung Lau, a man of Pengcheng, took a wife. But on their wedding night she produced a two-foot fish and said:

"You must love this carp as you do me."

Its eye swivelled to stare at Chung. He permitted her to keep it in the house. However three days later he was drunk and cooked the carp for his supper.

"Now we can never be together," said his wife. "But before I go, I will gift you ten gold coins. You must not spend them or a terrible curse will befall you."

Chung missed his wife but took up with a girl from the village. "What are these coins?" she asked, but Chung would not speak of his sadness. So she spent five of the coins on silks.

That night Chung was visited by a figure in an immense yellow hat. "I have come," it said, "to take you to the Kiosk of Sorrow, in the Hell of Yellow Suffering." But Chung would not go and the figure departed.

The following day he met a golden pheasant in the fields. It had one leg and one wing. "I thank you," said the pheasant as it tried to balance, "for you have released me from half of my sufferings. Spend the other five coins and I will grant you luck."

Chung returned home but could only find two gold coins. "A tax collector demanded one," said the girl from the village, "and I spent two more on this portrait."

The painting showed a woman staring at bamboo.

That night Chung lay with the girl from the village. As the moonlight touched her skin it became fur and he saw she was a tiger. "Think on all you have seen," she said, "then you will understand." With that she left him forever.

Chung arose at dawn and walked all the way into town, where he stopped at a tea house and drank three cups of tea. An old man challenged him to a game of auspicious wooden sticks but Chung did not play.

On the road home he saw a dragon winding its way through the fields. Chung was frightened but it changed into a beautiful girl. "Take this," she said, and gave him a piece of paper covered in elegant calligraphy. "One day you will meet a fox selling ginseng dumplings, and then everything will be clear." Chung asked the girl to come to his home for a meal, but she declined politely.

That night he examined her gift, but could not read the characters. Chung rolled it carefully but later became drunk and spilled wine all over the paper. Before sleep he looked west from his house and saw an immense warrior straddling the horizon, parting the clouds with his fiery beard.

In the morning while Chung was still drowsy, the one-legged golden pheasant came to him in great sorrow and leaned against the wall. "Did you not recognise your own father?" it asked. Upon which it fell from the wall, made a woeful noise, and died.

Ethernet

Yeah, I will have another. Thanks. A rough day? I don't know. It depends on your perspective. I shut someone down today, shut them down forever. And I do mean forever. Easy on the ice please. Thank you. *Slainte.*

I'm a network investigator. I work mostly for record companies. They pay me to locate kids swapping music on the Internet, then they sue the parents for thousands of pounds. In my day, I broke a couple of windows playing football and got clipped round the ear for it. Times change.

This week, they put me on to an IP address and I can't get my head round the profile. The perp is sharing AC/DC, Avril Lavigne and the Andrews Sisters. You know? Bucks Fizz, Busted and Barbra Streisand. What's that about?

I snoop on the traffic from that address and see he's updating a blog. I check it out. Most of these kids pretend they're vampires, but this one's different. He says he's a ghost.

It's all moan, moan, moan about how bored he is with the afterlife and `lt sUx dOOd`. He urges his readers to

`L1v 42 dAy`. I wonder if he is, at that moment, sitting in front of a webcam with a sheet over his head.

He's got a Flickr account, but there's no photos of him. It's all overexposed shots of people in HMV with strange smudges above their heads. He leaves comments like `th1s 14mer b0ught ka15er ch1ef$` and `b33tHoveN z gay`.

No surprise, he has a MySpace page. It's pimped so hard it's almost unreadable, with a background picture of a skeleton in a leather jacket riding a motorbike. He mostly seems to friend hot girls who upload pictures of themselves in their underwear, and posts asking if they're into necrophilia.

I listen to his music. All three tracks sound like a theremin with too much reverb.

Despite myself, I'm taken by the kid's consistency of image. Everything is pitched like he truly is a ghost. So instead of slamming the hammer down straight away, I go looking for him, and find him playing a text-based fantasy role-playing game. He's logged in as an elven sorceress. I go in as some kind of dwarf.

`This interface sucks`, I type, and watch the glowing screen.

`y w15h 1 h4d world of warcraft`, he responds.

`Are you really a ghost?`

A long pause.

`y 1t 15 teh sux0r`

`You sound kind of lonely.`

`y`

I stare at the little green letter.

`How did you manage to get an Internet connection?`

`1r a g3nu15`

I'm from the record company. They want me to stop you filesharing.

kekeke 1 hax0r3d ur t00n3z

You can't get away with it these days. They send guys like me to shut you down.

u n00b ur d0nkey pr0n

You could be a celebrity instead of stealing music. You could be the Net's first resident spectre. You'd be slashdotted. You could pass on messages to the afterlife and take commission by Paypal. Don't you want all that?

My cursor blinks. I count the seconds. Ten, twenty, thirty ... then his sorceress blasts my dwarf with a fireball and I get disconnected.

I feel kind of sad as I hit up his ISP for the incoming number. It leads to a disused office on the East Side. No lights. I'm ready to pick the locks when I notice the cemetery next door and the dilapidated telephone pole collapsed against a yew tree. Somehow, I'm not surprised.

The gates are closed, so I scale the rough wall. I already know what I'm going to find. The broken telephone wire trails through the muck and disappears into one particular plot. I approach the headstone from behind, acid in my guts.

I just don't know if I can do it. This kid died young, but he's still got some kind of a life, communicating with the living, even if it is through a semi-literate blog and third-rate games. Do I have the right to take that away because of a few stolen songs? Wouldn't it amount to killing him all over again?

DEARLY DEPARTED, says the inscription. BORN 1964. DIED 2007.

He was 43.

I rip the wire out of the ground and take it away with me.

8.15 to Doom

I crammed myself on to the Glasgow train at Waverley, amongst faces I saw every day. To my annoyance, the tables were all occupied and I took the window side of a cramped double seat. The carriage rumbled into motion as I opened my laptop in the confined space and tried to concentrate.

"You know, we're not getting out of here alive," said a voice from the seat beside me. I ignored it.

"This is our last journey on Earth," the voice said. I still ignored it.

"This line leads straight to Hell," it said. I gave up and looked.

He was a wee man, with a bushy brown beard in which I observed several sticky patches. He looked at me through huge spectacles. One lens was considerably thicker than the other, which gave the impression that one of his eyes was huge.

"Yes," he said, "I'm your co-passenger on the train to the afterlife."

"It's too early in the morning for this kind of rubbish," I said.

"Ah!" he said. "You mean it's too *late*. You thought you were taking your regular service. But this morning, sonny, you've boarded ... *a ghost train.*"

I looked around the carriage. Over the seat in front, two young men had linked their handheld computer games with a cable. Across the aisle, three commuters were reading today's *Financial Times*. A sleepy woman in a furry jacket probed her right ear with the blunt end of a pencil.

"It looks much the same," I said.

He leaned close and pushed his huge eye towards my face. "To you, perhaps. It takes special, spectral vision to see what's coming through the ether."

"How come you can see it?"

"Because..." He gave a cunning little smile. "...I'm a ghost too."

I poked him.

"Ow!" he said, and pulled back a bit.

"You seem fairly solid."

"Only the living would be arrogant enough to presume they know the ways of the dead." But he looked miffed. I smiled and returned to my laptop.

"That's right," he said. "You sit there. Ignore the facts. But within the hour, you and every other passenger on this terrible train will be dead."

We pulled into Haymarket station. Faces slipped past the window, lines of additional commuters who would soon be crowding on board to stand in the aisles. I was tempted for a moment, genuinely tempted, to vacate my seat and disembark. The next train would leave me only fifteen minutes late, and I would escape from the rantings of this awful man.

In truth, his warning had chilled me, irrational as it was. I had been raised on disaster movies, spooky stories of dread warnings and omens, and the terrible catastrophes which befell those who ignored them. I felt a primitive urge to grab my laptop, push past the tinpot prophet, and fight my way from the carriage through the ranks of incoming passengers.

However, the adult in me triumphed. The carriage filled and Haymarket began to slide away. I looked at the man beside me. He seemed possessed of a grim satisfaction.

"A hundred years ago, in 1904," he said, "the ways of rail were quite different. A second station, named 'Princes Street', served the passengers of the day, and the two westbound lines merged near Murrayfield. The stations were run by rival operators, and safety was sometimes overlooked in the pressures of competition.

"On that fateful morning, the 8.15 left Waverley just as it did today. And exactly four minutes later, a second train left Princes Street, ten minutes late."

He drew closer again and held up a finger. "By the regulations of the day, the Waverley train should have passed the points first while the Princes Street train was held back. But a crucial message didn't get through, and an inexperienced signalman failed to compensate.

"The points switched to admit the Princes Street train to the line, and it passed safely. But they stayed switched, and thirty seconds later, the 8.15 from Waverley passed through an 'all clear' signal and hit the mis-set points under full steam. Every man, woman and child on board was killed. It was a catastrophe to rival the Tay Bridge disaster."

I tried to interrupt, but my mouth was dry. He checked his watch and smiled gently. There was destiny on his brow.

"You see, there is an identical failure today. A simultaneous failure of points and signalling. And in just ninety seconds, this train will hit those misplaced points at full speed and derail in the worst Scottish rail accident for decades. You and everybody else here will make your departure from this life exactly a hundred years after the first disaster, on May the 13th, 2004."

I frowned.

"The 14th," I said. "This is May the 14th. Not the 13th."

"What?" he said.

About the Author

Gavin Inglis has variously been a handyman, teacher, punk DJ, journalist, busker, UNIX system administrator, stage manager, public relations executive and Jimmy Destri. He lives in Edinburgh's South Side with a squeaky skeleton and no cats.

His short stories have appeared in publications as diverse as *Scottish Book Collector, Son and Foe, Nova Scotia* and *Grunt and Groan: The New Fiction Anthology of Work and Sex.* Gavin's gothic novel for teenagers, *Mirror Widow,* won the "Instant Books" competition at the 2002 Edinburgh International Book Festival. In 2005 he received a bursary from the Scottish Arts Council. His website can be found at: www.gavininglis.com.

Gavin would like to thank the following people who made significant contributions to this edition of *Crap Ghosts:* Andrew J. Wilson, Lynn Findlay, Morag Edward, Andrew C. Ferguson, Frank and Mary Inglis, Gillian Jack and Kenny Inglis.

Special thanks are due to Lynn Holden for her inspiration and uncanny introduction.